TIGER BY THE TAIL!
TWO DOMINIC FLANDRY ADVENTURES

TIGER BY THE TAIL!
TWO DOMINIC FLANDRY ADVENTURES

POUL ANDERSON

SCIENCE FICTION CLASSICS

TIGER BY THE TAIL!

Published in 2009 by Science Fiction Classics. "Honorable Enemies" originally appeared in *Future Combined with Science Fiction Stories*, May 1951. "Tiger by the Tail" originally appeared in *Planet Stories*, November 1950-January 1951. No record of copyright renewals on file.

CONTENTS

Honorable Enemies. 7

Tiger by the Tail 33

HONORABLE ENEMIES

The door swung open behind him, and a voice murmured gently: "Good evening, Captain Flandry."

He spun around, grabbing for his stun pistol in a wild reflex, and found himself looking down the muzzle of a blaster. Slowly, then, he let his hands fall and stood taut, his eyes searching beyond the weapon, and the slender six-fingered hand that held it, to the tall gaunt body and the sardonically smiling face behind.

The face was humanoid — lean, hawk-nosed, golden-skinned, with brilliant amber eyes under feathery blue brows, and a high crest of shining blue feathers rising from the narrow hairless skull. The being was dressed in the simple white tunic of his people, leaving his clawed avian feet bare, but insignia of rank hung bejeweled around his neck and a cloak like a gush of blood from his wide shoulders.

But they'd all been occupied elsewhere — Flandry had seen to that. What had slipped up — ?

With an effort, Flandry relaxed and let a wry smile cross his face. Never mind who was to blame; he was trapped in the Merseian chambers and had to think of a way to escape with a whole skin. His mind whirred with thought. Memory came — this was Aycharaych of Chereion, who had come to join the Merseian embassy only a few days before, presumably on some mission corresponding to Flandry's.

"Pardon the intrusion," he said; "it was purely professional. No offense meant."

"And none taken," said Aycharaych politely. He spoke faultless Anglic, only the faintest hint of his race's harsh accent in the syllables. But courtesy between spies was meaningless. It would be too easy to blast down the intruder and later express his immense regret that he had shot down the ace intelligence officer of the Terrestrial Empire under the mistaken impression that it was a burglar.

Somehow, though, Flandry didn't think that the Chereionite would be guilty of such crudeness. His mysterious people were too old, too coldly civilized, and Aycharaych himself had too great a reputation for subtlety. Flandry had heard of him before; he would be planning something worse.

"That is quite correct," nodded Aycharaych. Flandry started — could the being guess his exact thoughts? "But if you will pardon my saying so, you yourself have committed a bit of clumsiness in trying to search our quarters. There are better ways of getting information."

Flandry gauged distances and angles. A vase on a table stood close to hand. If he could grab it up and throw it at Aycharaych's gun hand —

The blaster waved negligently. "I would advise against the attempt," said the Chereionite.

He stood aside. "Good evening, Captain Flandry," he said.

The Terran moved toward the door. He couldn't let himself be thrown out this way, not when his whole mission depended on finding out what the Merseians were up to. If he could make a sudden lunge as he passed close —

He threw himself sideways with a twisting motion that brought him under the blaster muzzle. Hampered by a greater gravity than the folk of his small planet were used to, Aycharaych couldn't dodge quickly enough. But he swung the blaster with a vicious precision across Flandry's jaw. The Terran stumbled, clasping the Chereionite's narrow waist. Aycharaych slugged him at the base of the skull and he fell to the floor.

He lay there a moment, gasping, blood running from his face. Aycharaych's voice jeered at him from a roaring darkness: "Really, Captain Flandry, I had thought better of you. Now please leave."

Sickly, the Terran crawled to his feet and went out the door.

Aycharaych stood in the entrance watching him go, a faint smile on his hard, gaunt visage.

Flandry went down endless corridors of polished stone to the suite given the Terrestrial mission. Most of them were at the feast, the ornate rooms stood almost empty. He threw himself into a chair and signaled his personal slave for a drink. A stiff one.

There was a light step and the suggestive whisper of a long

silkite skirt behind him. He looked around and saw Aline Chang-Lei, the Lady Marr of Syrtis, his partner on the mission and one of Sol's top field agents for intelligence.

She was tall and slender, dark of hair and eye, with the high cheekbones and ivory skin of a mixed heritage such as most Terrans showed these days; her sea-blue gown did little more than emphasize the appropriate features. Flandry liked to look at her, though he was pretty well immune to beautiful women by now.

"What was the trouble?" she asked at once.

"What brings you here?" he responded. "I thought you'd be at the party, helping distract everyone."

"I just wanted to rest for a while," she said. "Official functions at Sol get awfully dull and stuffy, but they go to the other extreme at Betelgeuse. I wanted to hear silence for a while." And then, with grave concern: "But you ran into trouble."

"How the hell it happened, I can't imagine," said Flandry "Look — we prevailed on the Sartaz to throw a brawl with everybody invited. We made double sure that every Merseian on the planet would be there. They'd trust to their robolocks to keep their quarters safe — they have absolutely no way of knowing that I've found a way to nullify a robolock. So what happens? I no sooner get inside than Aycharaych of Chereion walks in with a blaster in his hot little hand. He anticipates everything I try and finally shows me the door. Finis."

"Aycharaych — I've heard the name somewhere. But it doesn't sound Merseian."

"It isn't. Chereion is an obscure but very old planet in the Merseian Empire. Its people have full citizenship with the dominant race, just as our empire grants Terrestrial citizenship to many nonhumans. Aycharaych is one of Merseia's leading intelligence agents. Few people have heard of him, precisely because he is so good. I've never clashed with him before, though."

"I know whom you mean now," she nodded. "If he's as you say, and he's here on Alfzar, it isn't good news."

Flandry shrugged. "We'll just have to take him into account, then. As if this mission weren't tough enough!"

He got up and walked to the balcony window. The two moons

of Alfzar were up, pouring coppery light on the broad reach of the palace gardens. The warm wind blew in with scent of strange flowers that had never bloomed under Sol and they caught the faint sound of the weird, tuneless music which the monarch of Betelgeuse favored.

For a moment, as he looked at the ruddy moonlight and the thronging stars, Flandry felt a wave of discouragement. The Galaxy was too big. Even the four million stars of the Terrestrial Empire were too many for one man ever to know in a lifetime. And there were the rival imperia out in the darkness of space, Gorrazan and Ythri and Merseia, like a hungry beast of prey — Too much, too much. The individual counted for too little in the enormous chaos which was modern civilization. He thought of Aline — it was her business to know who such beings as Aycharaych were, but one human skull couldn't hold a universe; knowledge and power were lacking.

Too many mutually alien races; too many forces clashing in space, and so desperately few who comprehended the situation and tried their feeble best to help — naked hands battering at an avalanche as it ground down on them.

Aline came over and took his arm. Her face turned up to his, vague in the moonlight, with a look he knew too well. He'd have to avoid her, when or if they got back to Terra; he didn't want to hurt her but neither could he be tied to any single human.

"You're discouraged with one failure?" she asked lightly. "Dominic Flandry, the single-handed conqueror of Scothania, worried by one skinny bird-being?"

"I just don't see how he knew I was going to search his place," muttered Flandry. "I've never been caught that way before, not even when I was the worst cub in the Service. Some of our best men have gone down before Aycharaych. I'm convinced MacMurtrie's disappearance at Polaris was his work. Maybe it's our turn now."

"Oh, come off it," she laughed. "You must have been drinking sorgan when they told you about him."

"Sorgan?" His brows lifted.

"Ah, now I can tell you something you don't know." She was

trying desperately hard to be gay. "Not that it's very important; I only happened to hear of it while talking with one of the Alfzarian narcotics detail. It's a drug produced on one of the planets here — Cingetor, I think — with the curious property of depressing certain brain centers such that the victim loses all critical sense. He has absolute faith in whatever he's told."

"Hm. Could be useful in our line of work."

"Not very. Hypnoprobes are better for interrogation, and there are more reliable ways of producing fanatics. The drug has an antidote which also confers permanent immunity. So it's not much use, really, and the Sartaz has suppressed its manufacture."

"I should think our Intelligence would like to keep a little on hand, just in case," he said thoughtfully. "And of course certain nobles in all the empires, ours included, would find it handy for purposes of seduction."

"What are you thinking of?" she teased him.

"Nothing; I don't need it," he said smugly.

The digression had shaken him out of his dark mood. "Come on," he said. "Let's go join the party."

She went along at his side. There was a speculative look about her.

II

Usually the giant stars have many planets, and Betelgeuse, with forty-seven, is no exception. Of these, six have intelligent native races, and the combined resources of the whole system are considerable, even in a civilization used to thinking in terms of thousands of stars.

When the first Terrestrial explorers arrived, almost a thousand years previously, they found that the people of Alfzar had already mastered interplanetary travel and were in the process of conquering the other worlds — a process speeded up by their rapid adoption of the more advanced human technology. However, they had not attempted to establish an empire on the scale of Sol or Merseia, contenting themselves with maintaining hegemony over enough neighbor suns to protect their home. There had been clashes with the expanding powers around them, but generations of wily Sartazes had found it profitable to play their potential enemies off against each other; and the great states had, in turn, found it expedient to maintain Betelgeuse as a buffer against their rivals and against the peripheral barbarians.

But the gathering tension between Terra and Merseia had raised Betelgeuse to a position of critical importance. Lying squarely between the two great empires, she was in a position with her powerful fleet to command the most direct route between them and, if allied with either one, to strike at the heart of the other. If Merseia could get the alliance, it would very probably be the last preparation she considered necessary for war with Terra. If Terra could get it, Merseia would suddenly be in a deteriorated position and would almost have to make concessions.

So both empires had missions on Alfzar trying to persuade the Sartaz of the rightness of their respective causes and the immense profits to be had by joining. Pressure was being applied wherever possible; officials were lavishly bribed; spies were swarming through the system getting whatever information they could and — of course — being immediately disowned by their governments if they were caught.

It was normal diplomatic procedure, but its critical importance had made the Service send two of its best agents, Flandry and Aline, to Betelgeuse to do what they could in persuading the Sartaz, finding out his weaknesses, and throwing as many monkey wrenches as possible into the Merseian activities. Aline was especially useful in working on the many humans who had settled in the system long before and become citizens of the kingdom; quite a few of them held important positions in the government and the military. Flandry —

And now, it seemed, Merseia had called in her top spy, and the subtle, polite, and utterly deadly battle was on.

The Sartaz gave a hunting party for his distinguished guests. It pleased his sardonic temperament to bring enemies together under conditions where they had to be friendly to each other. Most of the Merseians must have been pleased, too; hunting was their favorite sport. The more citified Terrestrials were not at all happy about it, but they could hardly refuse.

Flandry was especially disgruntled at the prospect. He had never cared for physical exertion, though he kept in trim as a matter of necessity. And he had too much else to do.

Too many things were going disastrously wrong. The network of agents, both Imperial and bribed Betelgeusean — who ultimately were under his command — were finding the going suddenly rugged. One after another, they disappeared; they walked into Merseian or Betelgeusean traps; they found their best approaches blocked by unexpected watchfulness. Flandry couldn't locate the source of the difficulty, but since it had begun with Aycharaych's arrival, he could guess. The Chereionite was too damned smart to be true. Sunblaze, it just wasn't possible that anyone could have known about those Jurovian projects, or that Yamatsu's hiding place should have been discovered, or — And now this damned hunting party! Flandry groaned.

His slave roused him in the dawn. Mist, tinged with blood by the red sun, drifted through the high windows of his suite. Someone was blowing a horn somewhere, a wild call in the vague mysterious light, and he heard the growl of engines warming up.

"Sometimes," he muttered sourly, "I feel like going to the Emperor and telling him where to put our beloved Empire."

Breakfast made the universe slightly more tolerable. Flandry dressed with his usual finicky care in an ornate suit of skintight green and a golden cloak with hood and goggles, hung a needle gun and dueling sword at his waist, and let the slave trim his reddish-brown mustache to the micrometric precision he demanded. Then he went down long flights of marble stairs, past royal guards in helmet and corselet, to the courtyard.

The hunting party was gathering. The Sartaz himself was present, a typical Alfzarian humanoid — short, stocky, hairless, blue-skinned, with huge yellow eyes in the round, blunt-faced head. Other nobles of Alfzar and its fellow planets were present, more guardsmen, a riot of color in the brightening dawn. There were the members of the regular Terrestrial embassy and the special mission, a harried and unhappy looking crew. And there were the Merseians.

Flandry gave them all formal geetings. After all, Terra and

Merseia were nominally at peace, however many men were being shot and cities burning on the marches. His gray eyes looked sleepy and indifferent but they missed no detail of the enemy's appearance.

The Merseian nobles glanced at him with the thinly covered contempt they had for all humans. They were mammals, but with more traces of reptilian ancestry in them than Terrans showed. A huge-thewed two meters they stood, with a spiny ridge running from forehead to the end of the long, thick tail which they could use to such terrible effect in hand-to-hand battle. Their hairless skins were pale green, faintly scaled, but their massive faces were practically human. Arrogant black eyes under heavy brow ridges met Flandry's gaze with a challenge.

I can understand that they despise us, he thought. Their civilization is young and vigorous, its energies turned ruthlessly outward; Terra is old, satiated — decadent. Our whole policy is directed toward maintaining the galactic status quo, not because we love peace but because we're comfortable the way things are. We stand in the way of Merseia's dream of an all-embracing galactic empire. We're the first ones they have to smash.

I wonder — historically, they may be on the right side. But Terra has seen too much bloodshed in her history, has too wise and weary a view of life. We've given up seeking perfection and glory; we've learned that they're chimerical — but that knowledge is a kind of death within us.

Still — I certainly don't want to see planets aflame and humans enslaved and an alien culture taking up the future. Terra is willing to compromise; but the only compromise Merseia will ever make is with overwhelming force. Which is why I'm here.

A stir came in the streaming red mist, and Aycharaych's tall form was beside him. The Chereionite smiled amiably. "Good morning, Captain Flandry," he said.

"Oh — good morning," said Flandry, starting. The avian unnerved him. For the first time, he had met his professional superior, and he didn't like it.

But he couldn't help liking Aycharaych personally. As they stood waiting, they fell to talking of Polaris and its strange worlds, from which the conversation drifted to the comparative xenology of intelligent primitives throughout the galaxy. Aycharaych had a vast fund of knowledge and a wry humor matching Flandry's. When the horn blew for assembly, they exchanged the regretful glance of brave enemies. It's too bad we have to be on opposite sides. If things had been different —

But they weren't.

The hunters strapped themselves into their tiny one-man airjets. Each had a needle-beam projector in the nose, not too much armament when you hunted the Borthudian dragons. Flandry thought that the Sartaz would be more than pleased if the game disposed of some of his guests.

The squadron lifted into the sky and streaked northward for the mountains. Fields and forests lay in dissolving fog below them, and the enormous red disc of Betelgeuse was rising into a purplish sky. Despite himself, Flandry enjoyed the reckless speed and the roar of cloven air around him. It was godlike, this rushing over the world to fight the monsters at its edge.

In a couple of hours, they raised the Borthudian mountains, gaunt windy peaks rearing into the upper sky, the snow on their flanks like blood in the ominous light. Signals began coming over the radio; scouts had spotted dragons here and there, and jet after jet broke away to pursue them. Presently Flandry found himself alone with one other vessel.

As they hummed over fanged crags and swooping canyons, he saw two shadows rise from the ground and his belly muscles tightened. Dragons!

The monsters were a good ten meters of scaled, snake-like length, with jaws and talons to rend steel. Huge leathery wings bore them aloft, riding the wind with lordly arrogance as they hunted the great beasts that terrorized villagers but were their prey.

Flandry kicked over his jet and swooped for one of them. It grew monstrously in his sights. He caught the red glare of its eyes as it banked to meet him. No running away here; the dragons had never learned to be afraid. It rose against him.

He squeezed his trigger and a thin sword of energy leaped out to burn past the creature's scales into its belly. The dragon held to its collision course. Flandry rolled out of its way. The mighty wings clashed meters from him.

He had not allowed for the tail. It swung savagely and the blow shivered the teeth in his skull. The airjet reeled and went into a spin. The dragon stooped down on it and the terrible claws ripped through the thin hull.

Wildly, Flandry slammed over his controls, tearing himself loose. He barrel-rolled, metal screaming as he swung about to meet the charge. His needle beam lashed into the open jaws and the dragon stumbled in midnight. Flandry pulled away and shot again, flaying one of the wings.

He could hear the dragon's scream. It rushed straight at him, swinging with fantastic speed and precision as he sought to dodge. The jaws snapped together and a section of hull skin was torn from the framework. Wind came in to sear the man with numbing cold.

Recklessly, he dove to meet the plunging monster, his beam before him like a lance. The dragon recoiled. With a savage grin, Flandry pursued, slashing and tearing.

The torn airjet handled clumsily. In midflight, it lurched and the dragon was out of his sights. Its wings buffeted him and he went spinning aside with the dragon after him.

The damned thing was forcing him toward the cragged mountainside. Its peaks reached hungrily after him, and the wind seemed to be a demon harrying him closer to disaster. He swung desperately, aware with sudden grimness that it had become a struggle for life with the odds on the dragon's side.

If this was the end, to be shattered against a mountain and eaten by his own quarry — He fought for control.

The dragon was almost on him, rushing down like a thunderbolt. It could survive a collision, but the jet would be knocked to earth. Flandry fired again, struggling to pull free. The dragon swerved and came on in the very teeth of his beam.

Suddenly it reeled and fell aside. The other jet was on it from behind, raking it with deadly precision. Flandry thought briefly that the remaining dragon must be dead or escaped and now its hunter had come to his aid — all the gods bless him, whoever he was!

Even as he watched, the dragon fell to earth, writhing and snapping as it did. It crashed onto a ledge and lay still.

Flandry brought his jet to a landing nearby. He was shaking with reaction, but his chief emotion was a sudden overwhelming sadness. There went another brave creature down into darkness, wiped out by a senseless history that seemed only to have the objective of destroying. He raised a hand in salute as he grounded.

The other jet had already landed a few meters off. As Flandry opened his cockpit canopy, its pilot stepped out.

Aycharaych.

The man's reaction was almost instantaneous. Gratitude and honor had no part in the Service. Here was his greatest enemy, all unsuspecting, and it would be the simplest thing in the world to shoot him down. Aycharaych of Chereion, lost in a hunt for dangerous game, too bad — and remorse could come later, when there was time —

His needle pistol was halfway from the holster when Aycharaych's weapon was drawn. Through the booming wind, he heard the alien's quiet voice: "No."

He raised his own hands, and his smile was bitter. "Go ahead," he invited. "You've got the drop on me."

"Not at all," said Aycharaych. "Believe me, Captain Flandry, I will never kill you except in self-defense. But since I will always be forewarned of your plans, you may as well abandon them."

The man nodded, too weary to feel the shock of the revelation which was here. "Thanks," he said. "For saving my life, that is."

"You're too useful to die," replied Aycharaych candidly, "but I'm glad of it."

They took the dragon's head and flew slowly back toward the palace. Flandry's mind whirled with a gathering dismay.

There was only one way in which Aycharaych could have known of the murder plan, when it had sprung into instantaneous being. And that same fact explained how he knew of every activity and scheme the Terrestrials tried, and how he could frustrate every one of them while his own work went on unhampered.

Aycharaych could read minds!

III

Aline's face was white and tense in the red light that streamed into the room. "No," she whispered.

"Yes," said Flandry grimly. "It's the only answer."

"But telepathy — everyone knows its limitations —"

Flandry nodded. "The mental patterns of different races are so alien that a telepath who can sense them has to learn a different 'language' for every species — in fact, for every individual among non-telepathic peoples, whose minds, lacking mutual contact, develop purely personal thought-types. Even then it's irregular and unreliable. I've never let myself be studied by any telepath not on our side, so I'd always considered myself safe.

"But Chereion is a very old planet. Its people have the reputation among the more superstitious Merseians of being sorcerers. Actually, of course, it's simply that they've discovered certain things about the nervous system which nobody else suspects yet. Somehow, Aycharaych must be able to detect some underlying resonance-pattern common to all intelligent beings.

"I'm sure he can only read surface thoughts, those in the immediate consciousness. Otherwise he'd have found out so much from all the Terrans with whom he must have had contact that Merseia would be ruling Sol by now. But that's bad enough!"

Aline said drearily, "No wonder he spared your life; you've become the most valuable man on his side!"

"And not a thing I can do about it," said Flandry. "He sees me every day. I don't know what the range of his mind is — probably only a few meters; it's known that all mental pulses are weak and fade rapidly with distance. But in any case, every time he meets me he skims my mind, reads all my plans — I just can't help thinking about them all the time — and takes action to forestall them."

"We'll have to get the Imperial scientists to work on a thought screen."

"Of course. But that doesn't help us now."

"Couldn't you just avoid him, stay in your rooms —"

"Sure. And become a complete cipher. I have to get around, see my agents and the rulers of Betelgeuse, learn facts and keep my network operating. And every single thing I learn is just so much work done for Aycharaych — with no effort on his part." Flandry puffed a cigaret into lighting and blew nervous clouds of smoke. "What to do, what to do?"

"Whatever we do," said Aline, "it has to be fast. The Sartaz is getting more and more cool toward our people. While we blunder and fail, Aycharaych is working — bribing, blackmailing, influencing one key official after another. We'll wake up some fine morning to find ourselves under arrest and Betelgeuse the loyal ally of Merseia."

"Fine prospect," said Flandry bitterly.

The waning red sunlight streamed through his windows, throwing pools of dried blood on the floor. The palace was quiet, the nobles resting after the hunt, the servants scurrying about preparing the night's feast. Flandry looked around at the weird decorations, at the unearthly light and the distorted landscape beyond the windows. Strange world under a strange sun, and himself the virtual prisoner of its alien and increasingly hostile people. He had a sudden wild feeling of being trapped.

"I suppose I should be spinning some elaborate counterplot," he said hopelessly. "And then, of course, I'll have to go down to the banquet and let Aycharaych read every detail of it — every little thing I know, laid open to his eyes because I just can't suppress my own thoughts —"

Aline's eyes widened, and her slim hand tightened over his. "What is it?" he asked. "What's your idea?"

"Oh — nothing, Dominic, nothing." She smiled. "I have some direct contact with Sol and —"

"You never told me that."

"No reason for you to know it. I was just wondering if I should report this new trouble or not. Galaxy knows how those muddleheaded bureaucrats will react to the news. Probably yank us back and cashier us for incompetence."

She leaned closer and her words came low and urgent. "Go find Aycharaych, Dominic. Talk to him, keep him busy, don't let him come near me to interfere. He'll know what you're doing, naturally, but he won't be able to do much about it if you're as clever a talker as they say. Make some excuse for me tonight, too, so I don't have to attend the banquet — tell them I'm sick or something. Keep him away from me!"

"Sure," he said with a little of his old spirit. "But whatever you're hatching in that lovely head, be quick about it. He'll get at you mighty soon, you know."

He got up and left. She watched him go, with a dawning smile on her lips.

Flandry was more than a little drunk when the party ended. Wine flowed freely at a Betelgeusean banquet, together with music, food, and dancing girls of every race present. He had enjoyed himself — in spite of everything — most of all, he admitted, he'd enjoyed talking to Aycharaych. The being was a genius of the first order in almost every field, and it had been pleasant to forget the dreadfully imminent catastrophe for a while.

He entered his chambers. Aline stood by a little table, and the muted light streamed off her unbound hair and the shimmering robe she wore. Impulsively, he kissed her.

"Goodnight, honey," he said. "It was nice of you to wait for me."

She didn't leave for her own quarters. Instead, she held out one of the ornate goblets on the table. "Have a nightcap, Dominic," she invited.

"No, thanks. I've had entirely too many."

"For me." She smiled irresistibly. He clinked glasses with her and let the dark wine go down his throat.

It had a peculiar taste, and suddenly he felt dizzy, the room wavered and tilted under him. He sat down on his bed until it had passed, but there was an — oddness — in his head that wouldn't go away.

"Potent stuff," he muttered.

"We don't have the easiest job in the world," said Aline softly. "We deserve a little relaxation." She sat down beside him. "Just tonight, that's all we have. Tomorrow is another day, and a worse day."

He would never have agreed before, his nature was too cool and self-contained, but now it was all at once utterly reasonable. He nodded.

"And you love me, you know," said Aline.

And he did.

Much later, she leaned close against him in the dark, her hair brushing his cheek, and whispered urgently: "Listen, Dominic, I have to tell you this regardless of the consequences; you have to be prepared for it."

He stiffened with a return of the old tension. Her voice went on, a muted whisper in the night: "I've contacted Sol by courier robot and gotten in touch with Fenross. He has brains, and he saw at once what must be done. It's a poor way, but the only way.

"The fleet is already bound for Betelgeuse. The Merseians think most of our strength is concentrated near Llynathawr, but that's just a brilliant piece of deception — Fenross' work. Actually, the main body is quite near, and they've got a new energy screen that'll let them slip past the Betelgeusean cordon without being detected. The night after tomorrow, a strong squadron will land in Gunazar Valley, in the Borthudians, and establish a beachhead. A detachment will immediately move to occupy the capital and capture the Sartaz and his court."

Flandry lay rigid with shock. "But this means war!" he strangled. "Merseia will strike at once, and we'll have to fight Betelgeuse too."

"I know. But the Imperium has decided we'll have a better chance this way. Otherwise, it looks as if Betelgeuse will go to the enemy by default.

"It's up to us to keep the Sartaz and his court from suspecting the truth till too late. We have to keep them here at the palace. The capture of the leaders of an absolute monarchy is always a disastrous blow. Fenross and Walton think Betelgeuse will surrender before Merseia can get here.

"By hook or crook, Dominic, you've got to keep them unaware. That's your job; at the same time, keep on distracting Aycharaych, keep him off my neck."

She yawned and kissed him. "Better go to sleep now," she said. "We've got a tough couple of days ahead of us."

He couldn't sleep. He got up when she was breathing quietly and walked over to the balcony. The knowledge was staggering. That the Empire, the bungling decadent Empire, could pull such a stroke and hope to get away with it!

Something stirred in the garden below. The moonlight was dim red on the figure that paced between two Merseian bodyguards. Aycharaych!

Flandry stiffened in dismay. The Chereionite looked up and he saw the wise smile on the telepath's face. He knew.

In the following two days, Flandry worked as he had rarely worked before. There wasn't much physical labor involved, but he had to maintain a web of complications such that the Sartaz would have no chance for a private audience with any Merseian and would not leave the capital on one of his capricious journeys. There was also the matter of informing such Betelgeusean traitors as were on his side to be ready, and —

It was nerve-shattering. To make matters worse, something was wrong with him: clear thought was an effort; he had a new and disastrous tendency to take everything at face value. What had happened to him?

Aycharaych excused himself on the morning after Aline's revelation and disappeared. He was out arranging something hellish for the Terrans when they arrived, and Flandry could do nothing about it. But at least it left him and Aline free to carry on their own work.

He knew the Merseian fleet could not get near Betelgeuse before the Terrans landed. It is simply not possible to conceal the approximate whereabouts of a large fighting force from the enemy. How it had been managed for Terra, Flandry couldn't imagine. He supposed that it would not be too large a task force which was to occupy Alfzar — but that made its mission all the more precarious.

The tension gathered, hour by slow hour. Aline went her own way, conferring with General Bronson, the human-Betelgeusean officer whom she had made her personal property. Perhaps he could disorganize the native fleet at the moment when Terra struck. The Merseian nobles plainly knew what Aycharaych had found out; they looked at the humans with frank hatred, but they made no overt attempt to warn the Sartaz. Maybe they didn't think they could work through the wall of suborned and confused officials which Flandry had built around him — more likely, Aycharaych had suggested a better plan for them. There was none of the sense of defeat in them which slowly gathered in the human.

It was like being caught in spider webs, fighting clinging gray stuff that blinded and choked and couldn't be pulled away. Flandry grew haggard, he shook with nervousness, and the two days dragged on.

He looked up Gunazar Valley in the atlas. It was uninhabited and desolate, the home of winds and the lair of dragons, a good place for a secret landing — only how secret was a landing that Aycharaych knew all about and was obviously ready to meet?

"We haven't much chance, Aline," he said to her. "Not a prayer, really."

"We'll just have to keep going." She was more buoyant than he, seemed almost cheerful as time stumbled past. She stroked his hair tenderly. "Poor Dominic, it isn't easy for you."

The huge sun sank below the horizon — the second day, and tonight was the hour of decision. Flandry came out into the great conference hall to find it almost empty.

"Where are the Merseians, your Majesty?" he asked the Sartaz.

"They all went off on a special mission," snapped the ruler. He was plainly ill pleased with the intriguing around him, of which he would be well aware.

A special mission — O almighty gods!

Aline and Bronson came in and gave the monarch formal greeting. "With your permission, your Majesty," said the general, "I would like to show you something of great importance in about two hours."

"Yes, yes," mumbled the Sartaz and stalked out.

Flandry sat down and rested his head on one hand. Aline touched his shoulder gently. "Tired, Dominic?" she asked.

"Yeah," he said. "I feel rotten. Just can't think these days."

She signaled to a slave, who brought a beaker forward. "This will help," she said. He noticed sudden tears in her eyes. What was the matter?

He drank it down without thought. It caught at him, he gasped and grabbed the chair arms for support. "What the devil —"

It spread through him with a sudden coolness that ran along his nerves toward his brain. It was like the hand that Aline had laid on his head, calming, soothing — Clearing!

Suddenly he sprang to his feet. The whole preposterous thing stood forth in its raw grotesquerie — tissue of falsehoods, monstrosity of illogic!

The Fleet couldn't have moved a whole task force this close without the Merseian intelligence knowing of it. There couldn't be a new energy screen that he hadn't heard of. Fenross would never try so fantastic a scheme as the occupation of Betelgeuse before all hope was gone.

He didn't love Aline. She was brave and beautiful, but he didn't love her.

But he had. Three minutes ago, he had been desperately in love with her.

He looked at her through blurring eyes as the enormous truth grew on him. She nodded, gravely, not seeming to care that tears ran down her cheeks. Her lips whispered a word that he could barely catch.

"Goodbye, my dearest."

IV

They had set up a giant televisor screen in the conference hall, with a row of seats for the great of Alfzar. Bronson had also taken the precaution of lining the walls with royal guardsmen whom he could trust — long rows of flashing steel and impassive blue faces, silent and moveless as the great pillars holding up the soaring roof.

The general paced nervously up and down before the screen, looking at his watch unnecessarily often. Sweat glistened on his forehead. Flandry sat relaxed; only one who knew him well could have read the tension that was like a coiled spring in him. Only Aline seemed remote from the scene, too wrapped in her own thoughts to care what went on.

"If this doesn't work, you know, we'll probably be hanged," said Bronson.

"It ought to," answered Flandry tonelessly. "If it doesn't, I won't give much of a damn whether we hang or not."

He was prevaricating there; Flandry was most fond of living, for all the wistful half-dreams that sometimes rose in him.

A trumpet shrilled, high brassy music between the walls and up to the ringing rafters. They rose and stood at attention as the Sartaz and his court swept in.

His yellow eyes were suspicious as they raked the three humans.

"You said that there was to be a showing of an important matter," he declared flatly. "I hope that is correct."

"It is, your Majesty," said Flandry easily. He was back in his element, the fencing with words, the casting of nets to entrap minds. "It is a matter of such immense importance that it should have been revealed to you weeks ago. Unfortunately, circumstances did not permit that — as the court shall presently see — so your Majesty's loyal general was forced to act on his own discretion with what help we of Terra could give him. But if our work has gone well, the moment of revelation should also be that of salvation."

"It had better be," said the Sartaz ominously. "I warn you — all of you — that I am sick of the spying and corruption the empires have brought with them. It is about time to cut the evil growth from Betelgeuse."

"Terra has never wished Betelgeuse anything but good, your Majesty," said Flandry, "and as it happens, we can offer proof of that. If —"

Another trumpet cut off his voice, and the warder's shout rang and boomed down the hall: "Your Majesty, the Ambassador of the Empire of Merseia asks audience."

The huge green form of Lord Korvash of Merseia filled the doorway with a flare of gold and jewelry. And beside him — Aycharaych!

Flandry was briefly rigid with shock. If that opponent came into the game now, the whole plan might crash to ruin. It was a daring, precarious structure which Aline had built; the faintest breath of argument could dissolve it — and then the lightnings would strike!

One was not permitted to bear firearms within the palace, but the dueling sword was a part of full dress. Flandry drew his with a hiss of metal and shouted aloud: "Seize those beings! They mean to kill the Sartaz!"

Aycharaych's golden eyes widened as he saw what was in Flandry's mind. He opened his mouth to denounce the Terran — and leaped back in bare time to avoid the man's murderous thrust.

His own rapier sprang into his hand. In a whirr of steel, the two spies met.

Korvash the Merseian drew his own great blade in sheer reflex. "Strike him down!" yelled Aline. Before the amazed Sartaz could act, she had pulled the stun pistol he carried from the holster and sent the Merseian toppling to the floor.

She bent over him, deftly removing a tiny needle gun from her bodice and palming it on the ambassador. "Look, your Majesty," she said breathlessly, "he had a deadly weapon. We knew the Merseians planned no good, but we never thought they would dare —"

The Sartaz's gaze was shrewd on her. "Maybe we'd better wait to hear his side of it," he murmured.

Since Korvash would be in no position to explain his side for a good hour, Aline considered it a victory.

But Flandry — her eyes grew wide and she drew a hissing gasp as she saw him fighting Aycharaych. It was the swiftest, most vicious duel she had ever seen, leaping figures and blades that were a blur of speed, back and forth along the hall in a clamor of steel and blood.

"Stop them!" she cried, and raised the stunner.

The Sartaz laid a hand on hers and took the weapon away.

"No," he said. "Let them have it out. I haven't seen such a show in years."

"Dominic —" she whispered.

Flandry had always thought himself a peerless fencer, but Aycharaych was his match. Though the Chereionite was hampered by gravity, he had a speed and precision which no human could ever meet, his thin blade whistled in and out, around and under the man's guard to rake face and hands and breast, and he was smiling — smiling.

His telepathy did him little or no good. Fencing is a matter of conditioned reflex — at such speeds, there isn't time for conscious thought. But perhaps it gave him an extra edge, just compensating for the handicap of weight.

Leaping, slashing, thrusting, parrying, clang and clash of cold steel, no time to feel the biting edge of the growing weariness — dance of death while the court stood by and cheered.

Flandry's own blade was finding its mark; blood ran down Aycharaych's gaunt cheeks and his tunic was slashed to red ribbons. The Terran's plan was simple and the only one possible for him. Aycharaych would tire sooner, his reactions would slow — the thing to do was to stay alive that long!

He let the Chereionite drive him backward down the length of the hall, leap by leap, whirling around with sword shrieking in hand. Thrust, parry, riposte, recovery — whirr, clang! The rattle of steel filled the hall and the Sartaz watched with hungry eyes.

The end came as he was wondering if he would ever live to see Betelgeuse rise again. Aycharaych lunged and his blade pierced Flandry's left shoulder. Before he could disengage it, the man had knocked the weapon spinning from his hand and had his own point against the throat of the Chereionite.

The hall rang with the savage cheering of Betelgeuse's masters. "Disarm them!" shouted the Sartaz.

Flandry drew a sobbing breath. "Your Majesty," he gasped, "let me guard this fellow while General Bronson goes on with our show."

The Sartaz nodded. It fitted his sense of things.

Flandry thought with a hard glee: Aycharaych, if you open your mouth, so help me, I'll run you through.

The Chereionite shrugged, but his smile was bitter.

"Dominic, Dominic!" cried Aline, between laughter and tears.

General Bronson turned to her. He was shaken by the near ruin. "Can you talk to them?" he whispered. "I'm no good at it."

Aline nodded and stood boldly forth. "Your Majesty and nobles of the court," she said, "we shall now prove the statements we made about the treachery of Merseia.

"We of Terra found out that the Merseians were planning to seize Alfzar and hold it and yourselves until their own fleet could arrive to complete the occupation. To that end they are assembling this very night in Gunazar Valley of the Borthudian range. A flying squad will attack and capture the palace —"

She waited until the uproar had subsided. "We could not tell your Majesty or any of the highest in the court," she resumed coolly, "for the Merseian spies were everywhere and we had reason to believe that one of them could read your minds. If they had known anyone knew of their plans, they would have acted at once. Instead we contacted General Bronson, who was not high enough to merit their attention, but who did have enough power to act as the situation required.

"We planted a trap for the enemy. For one thing, we mounted telescopic telecameras in the valley. With your permission, I will now show what is going on there this instant."

She turned a switch and the scene came to life — naked crags and cliffs reaching up toward the red moons, and a stir of activity in the shadows. Armored forms were moving about, setting up atomic guns, warming the engines of spaceships — and they were Merseians.

The Sartaz snarled. Someone asked, "How do we know this is not a falsified transmission?"

"You will be able to see their remains for yourself," said Aline. "Our plan was very simple. We planted atomic land mines in the ground. They are radio controlled." She held up a small switchbox wired to the televisor, and her smile was grim. "This is the control. Perhaps your Majesty would like to press the button?"

"Give it to me," said the Sartaz thickly. He thumbed the switch.

A blue-white glare of hell-flame lit the screen. They had a vision of the ground fountaining upward, the cliffs toppling down, a cloud of radioactive dust boiling up toward the moons, and then the screen went dark.

"The cameras have been destroyed," said Aline quietly. "Now, your Majesty, I suggest that you send scouts there immediately. They will find enough remains to verify what the televisor has shown. I would further suggest that a power which maintains armed forces within your own territory is not a friendly one!"

Korvash and Aycharaych were to be deported with whatever other Merseians were left in the system — once Betelgeuse had broken diplomatic relations with their state and begun negotiating an alliance with Terra. The evening before they left, Flandry gave a small party for them in his apartment. Only he and Aline were there to meet them when they entered.

"Congratulations," said Aycharaych wryly. "The Sartaz was so furious he wouldn't even listen to our protestations. I can't blame him — you certainly put us in a bad light."

"No worse than your own," grunted Korvash angrily. "Hell take you for a lying hypocrite, Flandry. You know that Terra has her own forces and agents in the Betelgeusean System, hidden on wild moons and asteroids. It's part of the game."

"Of course I know it," smiled the Terran. "But does the Sartaz? However, it's as you say — the game. You don't hate the one who beats you in chess. Why then hate us for winning this round?"

"Oh, I don't," said Aycharaych. "There will be other rounds."

"You've lost much less than we would have," said Flandry. "This alliance has strengthened Terra enough for her to halt your designs, at least temporarily. But we aren't going to use that strength to launch a war against you, though I admit that we should. The Empire wants only to keep the peace."

"Because it doesn't dare fight a war," snapped Korvash.

They didn't answer. Perhaps they were thinking of the cities that would not be bombed and the young men that would not go out to be killed. Perhaps they were simply enjoying a victory.

Flandry poured wine. "To our future amiable enmity," he toasted.

"I still don't see how you did it," said Korvash.

"Aline did it," said Flandry. "Tell them, Aline."

She shook her head. She had withdrawn into a quietness which was foreign to her. "Go ahead, Dominic," she murmured. "It was really your show."

"Well," said Flandry, not loath to expound, "when we realized that Aycharaych could read our minds, it looked pretty hopeless. How can you possibly lie to a telepath? Aline found the answer — by getting information which just isn't true.

"There's a drug in this system called sorgan which has the property of making its user believe anything he's told. Aline fed me some without my knowledge and then told me that fantastic lie about Terra coming in to occupy Alfzar. And, of course, I accepted it as absolute truth. Which you, Aycharaych, read in my mind."

"I was puzzled," admitted the Chereionite. "It just didn't look reasonable to me; but as you said, there didn't seem to be any way to lie to a telepath."

"Aline's main worry was then to keep out of mind-reading range," said Flandry. "You helped us there by going off to prepare a warm reception for the Terrans. You gathered all your forces in the valley, ready to blast our ships out of the sky."

"Why didn't you go to the Sartaz with what you knew — or thought you knew?" asked Korvash accusingly.

Aycharaych shrugged. "I realized Captain Flandry would be doing his best to prevent me from doing that and to discredit any information I could get that high," he said. "You yourself agreed that our best opportunity lay in repulsing the initial attack ourselves. That would gain us far more favor with the Sartaz; moreover, since there would have been overt acts on both sides, war between Betelgeuse. and Terra would then have been inevitable — whereas if the Sartaz had learned in time of the impending assault, he might have tried to negotiate."

"I suppose so," said Korvash glumly.

"Aline, of course, prevailed on Bronson to mine the valley," said Flandry. "The rest you know. When you yourselves showed up —"

"To tell the Sartaz, now that it was too late," said Aycharaych.

" — we were afraid that the ensuing argument would damage our own show. So we used violence to shut you up until it had been played out." Flandry spread his hands in a gesture of finality. "And that, gentlemen, is that."

"There will be other tomorrows," said Aycharaych gently. "But I am glad we can meet in peace tonight."

The party lasted well on toward dawn. When the aliens left, with many slightly tipsy expressions of good will and respect, Aycharaych took Aline's hand in his own bony fingers. His strange golden eyes searched hers, even as she knew his mind was looking into the depths of her own.

"Goodbye, my dear," he said, too softly for the others to hear. "As long as there are women like you, I think Terra will endure."

She watched his tall form go down the corridor and her vision blurred a little. It was strange to think that her enemy knew what the man beside her did not.

TIGER BY THE TAIL

Captain Flandry opened his eyes and saw a metal ceiling. Simultaneously, he grew aware of the thrum and quiver which meant he was aboard a spaceship running on ultradrive.

He sat up with a violence that sent the dregs of alcohol swirling through his head. He'd gone to sleep in a room somewhere in the stews of Catawrayannis, with no prospect or intention of leaving the city for an indefinite time — let alone the planet! Now —

The chilling realization came that he was not aboard a human ship. Humanoid, yes, from the size and design of things, but no vessel ever built within the borders of the Empire, and no foreign make that he knew of.

Even from looking at this one small cabin, he could tell. There were bunks, into one of which he had fitted pretty well, but the sheets and blankets weren't of plastic weave. They seemed — he looked more closely — the sheets seemed to be of some vegetable fiber, the blankets of long bluish-gray hair. There were a couple of chairs and a table in the middle of the room, wooden, and they must have seen better days for they were elaborately handcarved in an intricate interwoven design new to Flandry — and planetary art-forms were a hobby of his. The way and manner in which the metal plating had been laid was another indication, and —

He sat down again, buried his whirling head in his hands, and tried to think. There was a thumping in his head and a vile taste in his mouth which liquor didn't ordinarily leave — at least not the stuff he'd been drinking — and now that he remembered, he'd gotten sleepy much earlier than one would have expected when the girl was so good-looking — Drugged — oh, no! Tell me I'm not as stupid as a stereofilm hero! Anything but that!

But who'd have thought it, who'd have looked for it? Certainly the people and beings on whom he'd been trying to get a lead would never try such a stunt. Besides, none of them had been around, he was sure of it. He'd simply been out building part of the elaborate structure of demimonde acquaintances and information which would eventually, by exceedingly indirect routes, lead him to those he was seeking. He'd simply been out having a good time — quite a good time, in fact — and —

And now someone from outside the Empire had him. And now what?

He got up, a little unsteadily, and looked around for his clothes. No sign of them. And he'd paid three hundred credits for that outfit, too. He stamped savagely over to the door. It didn't have a photocell attachment; he jerked it open and found himself looking down the muzzle of a blaster.

It was of different design from any he knew, but it was quite unmistakable. Captain Flandry sighed, relaxed his taut muscles, and looked more closely at the guard who held it.

He was humanoid to a high degree, perhaps somewhat stockier than Terrestrial average — and come to think of it, the artificial gravity was a little higher than one gee — and with very white skin, long tawny hair and beard, and oblique violet eyes. His ears were pointed and two small horns grew above his heavy eyebrow ridges, but otherwise he was manlike enough. With civilized clothes and a hooded cloak he could easily pass himself off for human.

Not in the getup he wore, of course, which consisted of a kilt and tunic, shining beryllium-copper cuirass and helmet, buskins over bare legs, and a murderous-looking dirk. As well as a couple of scalps hanging at his belt.

He gestured the prisoner back, and blew a long hollow blast on a horn slung at his side. The wild echoes chased each other down the long corridor, hooting and howling with a primitive clamor that tingled faintly along Captain Flandry's spine.

He thought slowly, while he waited: No intercom, apparently not even speaking tubes laid the whole length of the ship. And household articles of wood and animal and vegetable fibres, and that archaic costume there — They were barbarians, all right. But no tribe that he knew about.

That wasn't too surprising, since the Terrestrial Empire and the half-dozen other civilized states in the known Galaxy ruled over several thousands of intelligent races and had some contact with nobody knew how many thousands more. Many of the others were, of course, still planet-bound, but quite a few tribes along the Imperial borders had mastered a lot of human technology without changing their fundamental outlook on things. Which is what comes of hiring barbarian mercenaries.

The peripheral tribes were still raiders, menaces to the border planets and merely nuisances to the Empire as a whole. Periodically they were bought off, or played off against each other — or the Empire might even send a punitive expedition out. But if one day a strong barbarian race under a strong leader should form a reliable coalition — then vae victis!

A party of Flandry's captors, apparently officers, guardsmen, and a few slaves, came down the corridor. Their leader was tall and powerfully built, with a cold arrogance in his pale-blue eyes that did not hide a calculating intelligence. There was a golden coronet on his head, and the robes that swirled around his big body were rainbow-gorgeous. Flandry recognized some items as having been manufactured within the Empire. Looted, probably.

They came to a halt before him and the leader looked him up and down with a deliberately insulting gaze. To be thus surveyed in the nude could have been badly disconcerting, but Flandry was immune to embarrassment and his answering stare was bland.

The leader spoke at last, in strongly accented but fluent Anglic: "You may as well accept the fact that you are a prisoner, Captain Flandry."

They'd have gone through his pockets, of course. He asked levelly, "Just to satisfy my own curiosity, was that girl in your pay?"

"Of course. I assure you that the Scothani are not the brainless barbarians of popular Terrestrial superstition, though —" a bleak smile — "it is useful to be thought so."

"The Scothani? I don't believe I've had the pleasure —"

"You have probably not heard of us, though we have had some contact with the Empire. We have found it convenient to remain in obscurity, as far as Terra is concerned, until the time is ripe. But — what do you think caused the Alarri to invade you, fifteen years ago?"

Flandry thought back. He had been a boy then, but he had, of course, avidly followed the news accounts of the terrible fleets that swept in over the marches and attacked Vega itself. Only the hardest fighting at the Battle of Mirzan had broken the Alarri. Yet it turned out that they'd been fleeing still another tribe, a wild and mighty race who had invaded their own system with fire and ruin. It was a common enough occurrence in the turbulent barbarian stars; this one incident had come to the Empire's notice only because the refugees had tried to conquer it in turn. A political upheaval within the Terrestrial domain had prevented closer investigation before the matter had been all but forgotten.

"So you were driving the Alarri before you?" asked Flandry with as close an approximation to the right note of polite interest as he could manage in his present condition.

"Aye. And others. The Scothani have quite a little empire now, out there in the wilderness of the Galaxy. But, since we were never originally contacted by Terrestrials, we have, as I say, remained little known to them."

So — the Scothani had learned their technology from some other race, possibly other barbarians. It was a familiar pattern, Flandry could trace it out in his mind. Spaceships landed on the primitive world, the initial awe of the natives gave way to the realization that the skymen weren't so very different after all — they could be killed like anyone else; traders, students, laborers, mercenary warriors visited the more advanced worlds, brought back knowledge of their science and technology; factories were built, machines produced, and some local king used the new power to impose his rule on all his planet; and then, to unite his restless subjects, he had to turn their faces outward, promise plunder and glory if they followed him out to the stars — Only the Scothani had carried it farther than most. And lying as far from the Imperial border as they did, they could build up a terrible power without the complacent, politics-ridden Empire being more than dimly aware of the fact — until the day when — Vae victis!

II

"Let us have a clear understanding," said the barbarian chief. "You are a prisoner on a warship already light years from Llynathawr, well into the Imperial marches and bound for Scotha itself. You have no chance of rescue, and mercy depends entirely on your own conduct. Adjust it accordingly."

"May I ask why you picked me up?" Flandry's tone was mild.

"You are of noble blood, and a highranking officer in the Imperial intelligence service. You may be worth something as a hostage. But primarily we want information."

"But I —"

"I know." The reply was disgusted. "You're very typical of your miserable kind. I've studied the Empire and its decadence long enough to know that. You're just another worthless younger son, given a high-paying sinecure so you can wear a fancy uniform and play soldier. You don't amount to anything."

Flandry let an angry flush go up his cheek. "Look here —"

"It's perfectly obvious," said the barbarian. "You come to Llynathawr to track down certain dangerous conspirators. So you register yourself in the biggest hotel in Catawrayannis as Captain Dominic Flandry of the Imperial Intelligence Service, you strut around in your expensive uniform dropping dark hints about your leads and your activities — and these consist of drinking and gambling and wenching the whole night and sleeping the whole day!" A cold humor gleamed in the blue eyes. "Unless it is your intention that the Empire's enemies shall laugh themselves to death at the spectacle."

"If that's so," began Flandry thinly, "then why —"

"You will know something. You can't help picking up a lot of miscellaneous information in your circles, no matter how hard you try not to. Certainly you know specific things about the organization and activities of your own corps which we would find useful information. We'll squeeze all you know out of you! Then there will be other services you can perform, people within the Empire you can contact, documents you can translate for us, perhaps various liaisons you can make — eventually, you may even earn your freedom." The barbarian lifted one big fist. "And in case you wish to hold anything back, remember that the torturers of Scotha know their trade."

"You needn't make melodramatic threats," said Flandry sullenly.

The fist shot out, and Flandry fell to the floor with darkness whirling and roaring through his head. He crawled to hands and knees, blood dripping from his face, and vaguely he heard the voice: "From here on, little man, you are to address me as befits a slave speaking to a crown prince of Scotha."

The Terrestrial staggered to his feet. For a moment his fists clenched. The prince smiled grimly and knocked him down again. Looking up, Flandry saw brawny hands resting on blaster butts. Not a chance, not a chance.

Besides, the prince was hardly a sadist. Such brutality was the normal order among the barbarians — and come to think of it, slaves within the Empire could be treated similarly.

And there was the problem of staying alive.

"Yes, sir," he mumbled.

The prince turned on his heel and walked away.

They gave him back his clothes, though someone had stripped the gold braid and the medals away. Flandry looked at the soiled, ripped garments and sighed. Tailor-made — !

He surveyed himself in the mirror as he washed and shaved. The face that looked back was wide across the cheekbones, straight-nosed and square-jawed, with carefully waved reddish-brown hair and a mustache trimmed with equal attention. Probably too handsome, he reflected, wiping the blood from under his nose, but he'd been young when he had the plasti-cosmetician work on him. Maybe when he got out of this mess he should have the face made over to a slightly more rugged pattern to fit his years. He was in his thirties now, after all — getting to be a big boy, Dominic.

The fundamental bone structure of head and face was his own, however, and so were the eyes: large and bright, with a hint of obliquity, the iris of that curious gray which can seem any color, blue or green or black or gold. And the trim, medium-tall body was genuine too. He hated exercises, but went through a dutiful daily ritual since he needed sinews and coordination for his work. And, too, a man in condition was something to look at among the usually flabby nobles of Terra; he'd found his figure no end of help in making his home leaves pleasant.

Well, can't stand here admiring yourself all day, old fellow. He slipped blouse, pants, and jacket over his silkite undergarments, pulled on the sheening boots, tilted his officer's cap at an angle of well gauged rakishness, and walked out to meet his new owners.

The Scothani weren't such bad fellows, he soon learned. They were big brawling lusty barbarians, out for adventure and loot and fame as warriors; they had courage and loyalty and a wild streak of sentiment that he liked. But they could also fly into deadly rages, they were casually cruel to anyone that stood in their way, and Flandry acquired a not too high respect for their brains. It would have helped if they'd washed oftener, too.

This warship was one of a dozen which Cerdic, the crown prince, had taken out on a plundering cruise. They'd sacked a good many towns, even some on nominally Imperial planets, and on the way back had sent down a man in a lifeboat to contact Cerdic's agents on Llynathawr, which was notoriously the listening post of this sector of the Empire. Learning that there was something going on which a special agent from Terra had been investigating, Cerdic had ordered him picked up. And that was that.

Now they were homeward bound, their holds stuffed with loot and their heads stuffed with plans for further inroads. It might not have meant much, but — well — Cerdic and his father Penda didn't seem to be just ordinary barbarian chiefs, nor Scothania an ordinary barbarian nation.

Could it be that somewhere out there among the many stars someone had finally organized a might that could break the Empire? Could the Long Night really be at hand?

Flandry shoved the thought aside. He had too much to do right now. Even his own job at Llynathawr, important as it was, could and would be handled by someone else — though not, he thought a little sadly, with the Flandry touch — and his own immediate worry was here and now. He had to find out the extent of power and ambition of the Scothani; he had to learn their plans and get the information to Terra, and somehow spike them even a little. After that there might be time to save his own hide.

Cerdic had him brought to the captain's cabin. The place was a typical barbarian chief's den, with the heads of wild beasts on the walls and their hides on the floors, old shields and swords hung up in places of honor, a magnificent golden vase stolen from some planet of artists shining in a corner. But there were incongruous modern touches, a microprint reader and many bookrolls from the Empire, astrographic tables and computer, a vodograph. The prince sat in a massive carven chair, a silkite robe flung carelessly over his broad shoulders. He nodded with a certain affability.

"Your first task will be to learn Scothanian," he said without preliminary. "As yet almost none of our people, even nobles, speak Anglic, and there are many who will want to talk to you."

"Yes, sir," said Flandry. It was what he would most have desired.

"You had better also start organizing all you know so you can present it coherently," said the prince. "And I, who have lived in the Empire, will be able to check enough of your statements to tell whether you are likely speaking the truth." He smiled mirthlessly. "If there is reason to suspect you are lying, you will be put to the torture. And one of our Sensitives will then get at the truth."

So they had Sensitives, too. Telepaths who could tell whether a being was lying when pain had sufficiently disorganized his mind were as bad as the Empire's hypnoprobes.

"I'll tell the truth, sir," he said.

"I suppose so. If you cooperate, you'll find us not an ungrateful people. There will be more wealth than was ever dreamed of when we go into the Empire. There will also be considerable power for such humans as are our liaison with their race."

"Sir," began Flandry, in a tone of weak self-righteousness, "I couldn't think of —"

"Oh, yes, you could," said Cerdic glumly. "I know you humans. I traveled incognito throughout your whole Empire, I was on Terra itself. I posed as one of you, or when convenient as just another of the subject races. I know the Empire — its utter decadence, its self-seeking politicians and pleasure-loving mobs, corruption and intrigue everywhere you go, collapse of morals and duty-sense, decline of art into craft and science into stagnancy — you were a great race once, you humans, you were among the first to aspire to the stars and we owe you something for that, I suppose. But you're not the race you once were."

The viewpoint was biased, but enough truth lay in it to make Flandry wince. Cerdic went on, his voice rising: "There is a new power growing out beyond your borders, young peoples with the strength and courage and hopefulness of youth, and they'll sweep the rotten fragments of the Empire before them and build something new and better."

Only, thought Flandry, only first comes the Long Night, darkness and death and the end of civilization, the howling peoples in the ruins of our temples and a myriad petty tyrants holding their dreary courts in the shards of the Empire. To say nothing of the decline of good music and good cuisine, taste in clothes and taste in women and conversation as a fine art.

"We've one thing you've lost," said Cerdic, "and I think ultimately that will be the deciding factor. Honesty. Flandry, the Scothani are a race of honest warriors."

"No doubt, sir," said Flandry.

"Oh, we have our evil characters, but they are few and the custom of private challenges soon eliminates them," said Cerdic. "And even their evil is an open and clean thing, greed or lawlessness or something like that; it isn't the bribery and conspiracy and betrayal of your rotten politicians. And most of us live by our code. It wouldn't occur to a true Scothani to do a dishonorable thing, to break an oath or desert a comrade or lie on his word of honor. Our women aren't running loose making eyes at every man they come across; they're kept properly at home till time for marriage and then they know their place as mothers and houseguiders. Our boys are raised to respect the gods and the king, to fight, and to speak truth. Death is a little thing, Flandry, it comes to everyone in his time and he cannot stay it, but honor lives forever.

"We don't corrupt ourselves. We keep honor at home and root out disgrace with death and torture. We live our code. And that is really why we will win."

Battleships help, thought Flandry. And then, looking into the cold bright eyes: He's fanatic. But a hell of a smart one. And that kind makes the most dangerous enemy.

Aloud he asked, humbly: "Isn't any stratagem a lie, sir? Your own disguised travels within the Empire —"

"Naturally, certain maneuvers are necessary," said the prince stiffly. "Nor does it matter what one does with regard to alien races. Especially when they have as little honor as Terrestrials."

The good old race-superority complex, too. Oh, well.

"I tell you this," said Cerdic earnestly, "in the hope that you may think it over and see our cause is just and be with us. We will need many foreigners, especially humans, for liaison and intelligence and other services. You may still accomplish something in a hitherto wasted life."

"I'll think about it, sir," said Flandry.

"Then go."

Flandry got.

The ship was a good three weeks en route to Scotha. It took Flandry about two of them to acquire an excellent working knowledge of the language, but he preferred to simulate difficulty and complained that he got lost when talk was too rapid. It was surprising how much odd information you picked up when you were thought not to understand what was being said. Not anything of great military significance, of course, but general background, stray bits of personal history, attitudes and beliefs — it all went into the neat filing system which was Flandry's memory, to be correlated with whatever else he knew or learned into an astonishingly complete picture.

The Scothani themselves were quite friendly, eager to hear about the fabulous Imperial civilization and to brag of their own wonderful past and future exploits. Since there was obviously nothing he could do, Flandry was under the loosest guard and had virtually the freedom of the ship. He slept and messed with the warriors, swapped bawdy songs and dirty jokes, joined their rough-and-tumble wrestling matches to win surprised respect for his skill, and even became the close friend and confidant of some of the younger males.

The race was addicted to gambling. Flandry learned their games, taught them some of the Empire's, and before the trip's end had won back his stolen finery plus several other outfits and a pleasantly jingling purse. It was — well — he almost hated to take his winnings from these overgrown babies. It just never occurred to them that dice and cards could be made to do tricks.

The picture grew. The barbarian tribes of Scotha were firmly united under the leadership of the Frithian kings, had been for several generations. Theoretically it was an absolute monarchy, though actually all classes except the slaves were free. They had conquered at least a hundred systems outright, contenting themselves with exacting tribute and levies from most of these, and dominated all others within reach. Under Penda's leadership, a dozen similar, smaller barbarian states had already formed a coalition with the avowed purpose of invading the Empire, capturing Terra, destroying the Imperial military forces, and making themselves masters. Few of them thought beyond the plunder to be had, though apparently some of them, like Cerdic, dreamed of maintaining and extending the Imperial domain under their own rule.

They had a formidable fleet — Flandry couldn't find out its exact size — and its organization and technology seemed far superior to that of most barbarian forces. They had a great industry, mostly slave-manned with the Scothan overlords supervising. They had shrewd leaders, who would wait till one of the Empire's recurring political crises had reduced its fighting strength, and who were extremely well informed about their enemy. It looked — bad!

Especially since they couldn't wait too long. Despite the unequalled prosperity created by industry, tribute, and piracy, all Scotha was straining at the leash, nobles and warriors in the whole coalition foaming to be at the Empire's throat; a whole Galactic sector had been seized by the same savage dream. When they came roaring in — well, you never could tell. The Empire's fighting strength was undoubtedly greater, but could it be mobilized in time? Wouldn't Penda get gleeful help from two or three rival imperia? Couldn't a gang of utterly fearless fanatics plow through the mass of self-seeking officers and indifferent mercenaries that made up most of the Imperial power today?

Might not the Long Night really be at hand?

III

Scotha was not unlike Terra — a little larger, a little farther from its sun, the seas made turbulent by three small close moons. Flandry had a chance to observe it telescopically — the ship didn't have magniscreens — and as they swept in, he saw the mighty disc roll grandly against the Galactic star-blaze and studied the continents with more care than he showed.

The planet was still relatively thinly populated, with great forests and plains standing empty, archaic cities and villages huddled about the steep-walled castles of the nobles. Most of its industry was on other worlds, though the huge military bases were all on Scotha and its moons. There couldn't be more than a billion Scothani all told, estimated Flandry, probably less, and many of them would live elsewhere as overlords of the interstellar domain. Which didn't make them less formidable. The witless hordes of humankind were more hindrance than help to the Empire.

Cerdic's fleet broke up, the captains bound for their estates. He took his own vessel to the capital, Iuthagaar, and brought it down in the great yards. After the usual pomp and ceremony of homecoming, he sent for Flandry.

"What is your attitude toward us now?" he asked.

"You are a very likeable people, sir," said the Terrestrial, "and it is as you say — you are a strong and honest race."

"Then you have decided to help us actively?" The voice was cold.

"I really have little choice, sir," shrugged Flandry. "I'll be a prisoner in any case, unless I get to the point of being trusted. The only way to achieve that is to give you my willing assistance."

"And what of your own nation?"

"A man must stay alive, sir. These are turbulent times."

Contempt curled Cerdic's lip. "Somehow I thought better of

you," he said. "But you're a human. You could only be expected to betray your oaths for your own gain."

Surprise shook Flandry's voice. "Wasn't this what you wanted, sir?"

"Oh, yes, I suppose so. Now come along. But not too close — you make me feel a little sick."

They went up to the great gray castle which lifted its windy spires over the city, and presently Flandry found himself granted an audience with the King of Scothania.

It was a huge and dimlit hall, hung with the banners and shields of old wars and chill despite the fires that blazed along its length. Penda sat on one end, wrapped in furs against the cold, his big body dwarfed by the dragon-carved throne. He had his eldest son's stern manner and bleak eyes, without the prince's bitter intensity — a strong man, thought Flandry, hard and ruthless and able — but perhaps not too bright.

Cerdic had mounted to a seat on his father's right. The queen stood on his left, shivering a little in the damp draft, and down either wall reached a row of guardsmen. The fire shimmered on their breastplates and helmets and halberds; they seemed figures of legend, but Flandry noticed that each warrior carried a blaster too.

There were others in evidence, several of the younger sons of Penda, grizzled generals and councillors, nobles come for a visit. A few of the latter were of non-Scothan race and did not seem to be meeting exceptional politeness. Then there were the hangers-on, bards and dancers and the rest, and slaves scurrying about. Except for its size — and its menace — it was a typical barbarian court.

Flandry bowed the knee as required, but thereafter stood erect and met the king's eye. His position was anomalous, officially Cerdic's captured slave, actually — well, what was he? Or what could he become in time?

Penda asked a few of the more obvious questions, then said slowly: "You will confer with General Nartheof here, head of our intelligence section, and tell him what you know. You may also make suggestions if you like, but remember that false intentions will soon be discovered and punished."

"I will be honest, your majesty."

"Is any Terrestrial honest?" snapped Cerdic.

"I am," said Flandry cheerfully. "As long as I'm paid, I serve faithfully. Since I'm no longer in the Empire's pay, I must perforce look about for a new master."

"I doubt you can be much use," said Penda.

"I think I can, your majesty," answered Flandry boldly. "Even in little things. For instance, this admirably decorated hall is so cold one must wear furs within it, and still the hands are numb. I could easily show a few technicians how to install a radiant heating unit that would make it like summer in here."

Penda lifted his bushy brows. Cerdic fairly snarled: "A Terrestrial trick, that. Shall we become as soft and luxurious as the Imperials, we who hunt vorgari on ski?"

Flandry's eyes, flitting around the room, caught dissatisfied expressions on many faces. Inside, he grinned. The prince's austere ideals weren't very popular with these noble savages. If they only had the nerve to —

It was the queen who spoke. Her soft voice was timid: "Sire, is there any harm in being warm? I — I am always cold these days."

Flandry gave her an appreciative look. He'd already picked up the background of Queen Gunli. She was young, Penda's third wife, and she came from more southerly Scothan lands than Iuthagaar; her folk were somewhat more civilized than the dominant Frithians. She was certainly a knockout, with that dark rippling hair and those huge violet eyes in her pert face. And that figure too — there was a suppressed liveliness in her; he wondered if she had ever cursed the fate that gave her noble blood and thus a political marriage.

For just an instant their eyes crossed.

"Be still," said Cerdic.

Gunli's hand fell lightly on Penda's. The king flushed.

"Speak not to your queen thus, Cerdic," he said. "In truth this Imperial trick is but a better form of fire, which no one calls unmanly. We will let the Terrestrial make one."

Flandry bowed his most ironical bow. Cocking an eye up at the queen, he caught a twinkle. She knew.

Nartheof made a great show of blustering honesty, but there was a shrewd brain behind the hard little eyes that glittered in his hairy face. He leaned back and folded his hands behind his head and gave Flandry a quizzical stare.

"If it is as you say —" he began.

"It is," said the Terrestrial.

"Quite probably. Your statements so far check with what we already know, and we can soon verify much of the rest. If, then, you speak truth, the Imperial organization is fantastically good." He smiled. "As it should be — it conquered the stars, in the old days. But it's no better than the beings who man it, and everyone knows how venial and cowardly the Imperials are today."

Flandry said nothing, but he remembered the gallantry of the Sirian units at Garrapoli and the dogged courage of the Valatian Legion and — well, why go on? The haughty Scothani just didn't seem able to realize that a state as absolutely decadent as they imagined the Empire to be wouldn't have endured long enough to be their own enemy.

"We'll have to reorganize everything," said Nartheof. "I don't care whether what you say is true or not, it makes good sense. Our whole setup is outmoded. It's ridiculous, for instance, to give commands according to nobility and blind courage instead of proven intelligence."

"And you assume that the best enlisted man will make the best officer," said Flandry. "It doesn't necessarily follow. A strong and hardy warrior may expect more of his men than they can give. You can't all be supermen."

"Another good point. And we should eliminate swordplay as a requirement; swords are useless today. And we have to train mathematicians to compute trajectories and everything else." Nartheof grimaced. "I hate to think what would have happened if we'd invaded three years ago, as many hotheads wanted to do. We would have inflicted great damage, but that's all."

"You should wait at least another ten or twenty years and really get prepared."

"Can't. The great nobles wouldn't stand for it. Who wants to be duke of a planet when he could be viceroy of a sector? But we have a year or two yet." Nartheof scowled. "I can get my own service whipped into shape, with your help and advice. I have most of the bright lads. But as for some of the other forces — gods, the dunderheads they have in command! I've argued myself hoarse with Nornagast, to no use. The fool just isn't able to see that a space fleet the size of ours must have a special coordinating division equipped with semantic calculators and — The worst of it is, he's a cousin to the king, he ranks me. Not much I can do."

"An accident could happen to Nornagast," murmured Flandry.

"Eh?" Nartheof gasped. "What do you mean?"

"Nothing," said Flandry lightly. "But just for argument's sake, suppose — well, suppose some good swordsman should pick a quarrel with Nornagast. I don't doubt he has many enemies. If he should unfortunately be killed in the duel, you might be able to get to his majesty immediately after, before anyone else, and persuade him to appoint a more reasonable successor. Of course, you'd have to know in advance that there'd be a duel."

"Of all the treacherous, underhanded — !"

"I haven't done anything but speculate," said Flandry mildly. "However, I might remind you of your own remarks. It's hardly fair that a fool should have command and honor and riches instead of better men who simply happen to be of lower degree. Nor, as you yourself said, is it good for Scothania as a whole."

"I won't hear of any such Terrestrial vileness."

"Of course not. I was just — well, speculating. I can't help it. All Terrestrials have dirty minds. But we did conquer the stars once."

"A man might go far, if only — no!" Nartheof shook himself. "A warrior doesn't bury his hands in muck."

"No. But he might use a pitchfork. Tools don't mind dirt. The man who wields them doesn't even have to know the details . . . But let's get back to business." Flandry relaxed even more lazily. "Here's a nice little bit of information which only highly placed Imperials know. The Empire has a lot of arsenals and munitions dumps which are guarded by nothing but secrecy. The Emperor doesn't dare trust certain units to guard such sources of power, and he can't spare enough reliable legions to watch them all. So obscure, uninhabited planets are used." Nartheof's eyes were utterly intent now. "I know of only one, but it's a good prospect. An uninhabited, barren system not many parsecs inside the border, the second planet honeycombed with underground works that are crammed with spaceships, atomic bombs, fuel — power enough to wreck a world. A small, swift fleet could get there, take most of the stores, and destroy the rest before the nearest garrison could ever arrive in defense."

"Is that true?"

"You can easily find out. If I'm lying, it'll cost you that small unit, that's all — and I assure you I've no desire to be tortured to death."

"Holy gods!" Nartheof quivered. "I've got to tell Cerdic now, right away —"

"You could. Or you might simply go there yourself without telling anyone. If Cerdic knows, he'll be the one to lead the raid. If you went, you'd get the honor — and the power —"

"Cerdic would not like it."

"Too late then. He could hardly challenge you for so bold and successful a stroke."

"And he is getting too proud of himself. He could stand a little taking down." Nartheof chuckled, a deep vibration in his shaggy breast. "Aye, by Valtam's beard, I'll do it! Give me the figures now —"

Presently the general looked up from the papers and gave Flandry a puzzled stare. "If this is the case, and I believe it is," he said slowly, "it'll be a first-rate catastrophe for the Empire. Why are you with us, human?"

"Maybe I've decided I like your cause a little better," shrugged Flandry. "Maybe I simply want to make the best of my own situation. We Terrestrials are adaptable beasts. But I have enemies here, Nartheof, and I expect to make a few more. I'll need a powerful friend."

"You have one," promised the barbarian. "You're much too useful to me to be killed. And — and — damn it, human, somehow I can't help liking you."

IV

The dice rattled down onto the table and came to a halt. Prince Torric swore good-naturedly and shoved the pile of coins toward Flandry. "I just can't win," he laughed. "You have the gods with you, human."

For a slave, I'm not doing so badly, thought Flandry. In fact, I'm getting rich. "Fortune favors the weak, highness," he smiled. "The strong don't need luck."

"To Theudagaar with titles," said the young warrior. He was drunk; wine flushed his open face and spread in puddles on the table before him. "We're too good friends by now, Dominic. Ever since you got my affairs in order —"

"I have a head for figures, and of course Terrestrial education helps — Torric. But you need money."

"There'll be enough for all when we hold the Empire. I'll have a whole system to rule, you know."

Flandry pretended surprise. "Only a system? After all, a son of King Penda —"

"Cerdic's doing," Torric scowled blackly. "The dirty avagar persuaded Father that only one — himself, of course — should succeed to the throne. He said no kingdom ever lasted when the sons divided power equally."

"It seems very unfair. And how does he know he's the best?"

"He's the oldest. That's what counts. And he's conceited enough to be sure of it." Torric gulped another beakerful.

"The Empire has a better arrangement. Succession is by ability alone, among many in a whole group of families."

"Well — the old ways — what can I do?"

"That's hardly warrior's talk, Torric. Admitting defeat so soon — I thought better of you!'

"But what to do — ?"

"There are ways. Cerdic's power, like that of all chiefs, rests on his many supporters and his own household troops. He isn't well liked. It wouldn't be hard to get many of his friends to give allegiance elsewhere."

"But — treachery — would you make a brotherslayer of me?"

"Who said anything about killing? Just — dislodging, let us say. He could always have a system or two to rule, just as he meant to give you."

"But — look, I don't know anything about your sneaking Terrestrial ways. I suppose you mean to dish — disaffect his allies, promise them more than he gives . . . What's that word — bribery? I don't know a thing about it, Dominic. I couldn't do it."

"You wouldn't have to do it," murmured Flandry. "I could help. What's a man for, if not to help his friends?"

Earl Morgaar, who held the conquered Zanthudian planets in fief, was a noble of power and influence beyond his station. He was also notoriously greedy.

He said to Captain Flandry: "Terrestrial, your suggestions about farming out tax-gathering have more than doubled my income. But now the natives are rising in revolt against me, murdering my troops wherever they get a chance and burning their farms rather than pay the levies. What do they do about that in the Empire?"

"Surely, sir, you could crush the rebels with little effort," said Flandry.

"Oh, aye, but dead men don't pay tribute either. Isn't there a better way? My whole domain is falling into chaos."

"Several ways, sir." Flandry sketched a few of them — puppet native committees, propaganda shifting the blame onto some scapegoat, and the rest of it. He did not add that these methods work only when skillfully administered.

"It is well," rumbled the earl at last. His hard gaze searched Flandry's impassively smiling face. "You've made yourself useful to many a Scothanian leader since coming here, haven't you? There's that matter of Nartheof — he's a great man now because he captured that Imperial arsenal. And there are others. But it seems much of this gain is at the expense of other Scothani, rather than of the Empire. I still wonder about Nornagast's death."

"History shows that the prospect of great gain always stirs up internal strife, sir," said Flandry. "It behooves the strong warrior to seize a dominant share of power for himself and so reunite his people against their common enemy. Thus did the early Terrestrial emperors end the civil wars and become the rulers of the then accessible universe."

"Ummm — yes. Gain — power — wealth — aye, some good warrior —"

"Since we are alone, sir," said Flandry, "perhaps I may remark that Scotha itself has seen many changes of dynasty."

"Yes — of course, I took an oath to the king. But suppose, just suppose the best interests of Scothania were served by a newer and stronger family —"

They were into details of the matter within an hour. Flandry suggested that Prince Kortan would be a valuable ally — but beware of Torric, who had ambitions of his own.

There was a great feast given at the winter solstice. The town and the palace blazed with light and shouted with music and drunken laughter. Warriors and nobles swirled their finest robes about them and boasted of the ruin they would wreak in the Empire. It was to be noted that the number of alcoholic quarrels leading to bloodshed was unusually high this year, especially among the upper classes.

There were enough dark corners, though. Flandry stood in one, a niche leading to a great open window, and looked over the glittering town lights to the huge white hills that lay silent beyond, under the hurtling moons. Above were the stars, bright with the frosty twinkle of winter; they seemed so near that one could reach a hand up and pluck them from the sky. A cold breeze wandered in from outside. Flandry wrapped his cloak more tightly about him.

A light footfall sounded on the floor. He looked about and saw Gunli the queen. Her tall young form was vague in the shadow, but a shaft of moonlight lit her face with an unearthly radiance. She might have been a lovely girl of Terra, save for the little horns and — well —

These people aren't really human. They look human, but no people of Terra were ever so — simple-minded! Then with an inward grin: *But you don't expect a talent for intrigue in women, Terrestrial or Scothan. So the females of this particular species are quite human enough for anyone's taste.*

The cynical mirth faded into an indefinable sadness. He — damn it, he liked Gunli. They had laughed together often in the last few months, and she was honest and warm-hearted and — well, no matter, no matter.

"Why are you here all alone, Dominic?" she asked. Her voice was very quiet, and her eyes seemed huge in the cold pale moonlight.

"It would hardly be prudent for me to join the party," he answered wryly. "I'd cause too many fights. Half of them out there hate my insides."

"And the other half can't do without you," she smiled. "Well I'm as glad not to be there myself. These Frithians are savages. At home —" She looked out the window and sudden tears glittered in her eyes.

"Don't weep, Gunli," said Flandry softly. "Not tonight. This is the night the sun turns, remember. There is always new hope in a new year."

"I can't forget the old years," she said with a bitterness that shocked him.

Understanding came. He asked quietly: "There was someone else, wasn't there?"

"Aye. A young knight. But he was of low degree, so they married me off to Penda, who is old and chill. And Jomana was killed in one of Cerdic's raids —" She turned her head to look at him, and a pathetic attempt at a smile quivered on her lips. "It isn't Jomana, Dominic. He was very dear to me, but even the deepest wounds heal with time. But I think of all the other young men, and their sweethearts —"

"It's what the men want themselves."

"But not what the women want. Not to wait and wait and wait till the ships come back, never knowing whether there will only be his shield aboard. Not to rock her baby in her arms and know that in a few years he will be a stiffened corpse on the shores of some unknown planet. Not — well —" She straightened her slim shoulders. "Little I can do about it."

"You are a very brave and lovely woman, Gunli," said Flandry. "Your kind has changed history ere this." And he sang softly a verse he had made in the Scothan bardic form:

> *"So I see you standing,*
> *sorrowful in darkness.*
> *But the moonlight's broken*
> *by your eyes tear-shining —*
> *moonlight in the maiden's*
> *magic net of tresses.*
> *Gods gave many gifts, but,*
> *Gunli, yours was greatest."*

Suddenly she was in his arms . . .

Sviffash of Sithafar was angry. He paced up and down the secret chamber, his tail lashing about his bowed legs, his fanged jaws snapping on the accented Scothanian words that poured out.

"Like a craieex they treat me!" he hissed. "I, king of a planet and an intelligent species, must bow before the dirty barbarian Penda. Our ships have the worst positions in the fighting line and the last chance at loot. The swaggering Scothani on Sithafar treat my people as if they were conquered peasants, not warrior allies. It is not to be endured!"

Flandry remained respectfully silent. He had carefully nursed the reptile king's smoldering resentment along ever since the being had come to Iuthagaar for conference, but he wanted Sviffash to think it was all his own idea.

"By the Dark God, if I had a chance I think I'd go over to the Terran side!" exploded Sviffash. "You say they treat their subjects decently?"

"Aye, we've learned it doesn't pay to be prejudiced about race, your majesty. In fact, many nonhumans hold Terrestrial citizenship. And of course a vassal of the Empire remains free within his own domain, except in certain matters of trade and military force where we must have uniformity. And he has the immeasurable power and wealth of the Empire behind and with him."

"My own nobles would follow gladly enough," said Sviffash. "They'd sooner loot Scothanian than Terrestrial planets, if they didn't fear Penda's revenge."

"Many other of Scotha's allies feel likewise, your majesty. And still more would join an uprising just for the sake of the readily available plunder, if only they were sure the revolt would succeed. It is a matter of getting them all together and agreeing —"

"And you have contacts everywhere, Terrestrial. You're like a spinner weaving its web. Of course, if you're caught I shall certainly insist I never had anything to do with you."

"Naturally, your majesty."

"But if it works — hah!" The lidless black eyes glittered and a forked tongue flickered out between the horny lips. "Hah, the sack of Scotha!"

"No, your majesty. It is necessary that Scotha be spared. There will be enough wealth to be had on her province planets."

"Why?" The question was cold, emotionless.

"Because you see, your majesty, we will have Scothan allies who will cooperate only on that condition. Some of the power-seeking nobles . . . and then there is a southern nationalist movement which wishes separation from the Frithian north . . . and I may say that it has the secret leadership of the queen herself . . ."

Flandry's eyes were as chill as his voice: "It will do you no good to kill me, Duke Asdagaar. I have left all the evidence with a reliable person who, if I do not return alive, or if I am killed later, will take it directly to the king and the people."

The Scothan's hands clenched white about the arms of his chair. Impotent rage shivered in his voice: "You devil! You crawling worm!"

"Name-calling is rather silly coming from one of your history," said Flandry. "A parricide, a betrayer of comrades, a breaker of oaths, a mocker of the gods — I have all the evidence, Duke Asdagaar. Some of it is on paper, some is nothing but the names of scattered witnesses and accomplices each of whom knows a little of your career. And a man without honor, on Scotha, is better dead. In fact, he soon will be."

"But how did you learn?" Hopelessness was coming into the duke's tone; he was beginning to tremble a little.

"I have my ways. For instance, I learned quite a bit by cultivating the acquaintance of your slaves and servants. You highborn forget that the lower classes have eyes and ears, and that they talk among themselves."

"Well —" The words were almost strangled. "What do you want?"

"Help for certain others. You have powerful forces at your disposal —"

Spring winds blew softly through the garden and stirred the trees to rustling. There was a deep smell of green life about them; a bird was singing somewhere in the twilight, and the ancient promise of summer stirred in the blood.

Flandry tried to relax in the fragrant evening, but he was too tense. His nerves were drawn into quivering wires and he had grown thin and hollow-eyed. So too had Gunli, but it seemed only to heighten her loveliness; it had more than a hint of the utterly alien and remote now.

"Well, the spaceship is off," said the man. His voice was weary. "Aethagir shouldn't have any trouble getting to Ifri, and he's a clever lad. He'll find a way to deliver my letter to Admiral Walton." He scowled, and a nervous tic began over his left eye. "But the timing is so desperately close. If our forces strike too soon, or too late, it can be ruinous."

"I don't worry about that, Dominic," said Gunli. "You know how to arrange these things."

"I've never handled an empire before, my beautiful. The next several days will be touch and go. And that's why I want you to leave Scotha now. Take a ship and some trusty guards and go to Alagan or Gimli or some other out-of-the-way planet." He smiled with one corner of his mouth. "It would be a bitter victory if you died in it, Gunli."

Her voice was haunted. "I should die. I've betrayed my lord — I am dishonored —"

"You've saved your people — your own southerners, and ultimately all Scotha."

"But the broken oaths —" She began to weep, quietly and hopelessly.

"An oath is only a means to an end. Don't let the means override the end."

"An oath is an oath. But Dominic — it was a choice of standing by Penda or by — you —"

He comforted her as well as he could. And he reflected grimly that he had never before felt himself so thoroughly a skunk.

The battle in space was, to the naked eye, hardly visible-brief flashes of radiation among the swarming stars, occasionally the dark form of a ship slipping by and occulting a wisp of the Milky Way. But Admiral Walton smiled with cold satisfaction at the totality of reports given him by the semantic integrator.

"We're mopping them up," he said. "Our task force has twice their strength, and they're disorganized and demoralized anyway."

"Whom are we fighting?" wondered Chang, the executive officer.

"Don't know for sure. They've split into so many factions you can never tell who it is. But from Flandry's report, I'd say it was — what was that outlandish name now? — Duke Markagrav's fleet. He holds this sector, and is a royalist. But it might be Kelry, who's also anti-Terrestrial — but at war with Markagrav and in revolt against the king."

"Suns and comets and little green asteroids!" breathed Chang. "This Scothanian hegemony seems just to have disintegrated. Chaos! Everybody at war with everybody else, and hell take the hindmost! How'd he do it?"

"I don't know." Walton grinned. "But Flandry's the Empire's ace secret service officer. He works miracles before breakfast. Why, before these barbarians snatched him he was handling the Llynathawr trouble all by himself. And you know how he was doing it? He went there with everything but a big brass band, did a perfect imitation of a political appointee using the case as an excuse to do some high-powered roistering, and worked his way up toward the conspirators through the underworld characters he met in the course of it. They never dreamed he was any kind of danger — as we found out after a whole squad of men had worked for six months to crack the case of his disappearance."

"Then the Scothanians have been holding the equivalent of a whole army, and didn't know it!"

"That's right," nodded Walton. "The biggest mistake they ever made was to kidnap Captain Flandry. They should have played safe and kept some nice harmless cobras for pets!"

Iuthagaar was burning. Mobs rioted in the streets and howled with fear and rage and the madness of catastrophe.

The remnants of Penda's army had abandoned the town and were fleeing northward before the advancing southern rebels. They would be harried by Torric's guerrillas, who in turn were the fragments of a force smashed by Earl Morgaar after Penda was slain by Kortan's assassins. Morgaar himself was dead and his rebels broken by Nartheof. The earl's own band had been riddled by corruption and greed and had fallen apart before the royalists' counterblow.

But Nartheof was dead too, at the hands of Nornagast's vengeful relatives. His own seizure of supreme power and attempt at reorganization had created little but confusion, which grew worse when he was gone. Now the royalists were a beaten force somewhere out in space, savagely attacked by their erstwhile allies, driven off the revolting conquered planets, and swept away before the remorselessly advancing Terrestrial fleet.

The Scothanian empire had fallen into a hundred shards, snapping at each other and trying desperately to retrieve their own with no thought for the whole. Lost in an incomprehensibly complex network of intrigue and betrayal, the great leaders fell, or pulled out of the mess and made hasty peace with Terra. War and anarchy flamed between the stars — but limited war, a petty struggle really. The resources and organization for real war and its attendant destruction just weren't there any more.

A few guards still held the almost deserted palace, waiting for the Terrestrials to come and end the strife. There was nothing they could do but wait.

Captain Flandry stood at a window and looked over the city. He felt no great elation. Nor was he safe yet. Cerdic was loose somewhere on the planet, and Cerdic had undoubtedly guessed who was responsible.

Gunli came to the human. She was very pale. She hadn't expected Penda's death and it had hurt her. But there was nothing to do now but go through with the business.

"Who would have thought it?" she whispered. "Who would have dreamed we would ever come to this? That mighty Scotha would lie at the conqueror's feet?"

"I would," said Flandry tonelessly. "Such jerry-built empires as yours never last. Barbarians just don't have the talent and the knowledge to run them. Being only out for plunder, they don't really build.

"Of course, Scotha was especially susceptible to this kind of sabotage. Your much-vaunted honesty was your own undoing. By carefully avoiding any hint of dishonorable actions, you became completely ignorant of the techniques and the preventive measures. Your honor was never more than a latent ability for dishonor. All I had to do, essentially, was to point out to your key men the rewards of betrayal. If they'd been really honest, I'd have died at the first suggestion. Instead, they grabbed at the chance. So it was easy to set them against each other until no one knew whom he could trust." He smiled humorlessly. "Not many Scothani objected to bribery or murder or treachery when it was shown to be to their advantage. I assure you, most Terrestrials would have thought further, been able to see beyond their own noses and realized the ultimate disaster it would bring."

"Still — honor is honor, and I have lost mine and so have all my people." Gunli looked at him with a strange light in her eyes. "Dominic, disgrace can only be wiped out in blood."

He felt a sudden tightening of his nerves and muscles, an awareness of something deadly rising before him. "What do you mean?"

She had lifted the blaster from his holster and skipped out of reach before he could move. "No — stay there!" Her voice was shrill. "Dominic, you are a cunning man. But are you a brave one?"

He stood still before the menace of the weapon. "I think —" He groped for words. No, she wasn't crazy. But she wasn't really human, and she had the barbarian's fanatical code in her as well. Easy, easy, or death would spit at him. "I think I took a few chances, Gunli."

"Aye. But you never fought. You haven't stood up man to man and battled as a warrior should." Pain racked her thin lovely face. She was breathing hard now. "It's for you as well as him, Dominic. He has to have his chance to avenge his father — himself — fallen Scotha — and you have to have a chance too. If you can win, then you are the stronger and have the right."

Might makes right. It was, after all, the one unbreakable law of Scotha. The old trial by combat, here on a foreign planet many light-years from green Terra —

Cerdic came in. He had a sword in either hand, and there was a savage glee in his bloodshot eyes.

"I let him in, Dominic," said Gunli. She was crying now. "I had to. Penda was my lord — but kill him, kill him!"

With a convulsive movement, she threw the blaster out of the window. Cerdic gave her an inquiring look. Her voice was almost inaudible: "I might not be able to stand it. I might shoot you, Cerdic."

"Thanks!" He ripped the word out, savagely. "I'll deal with you later, traitress. Meanwhile —" A terrible laughter bubbled in his throat — "I'll carve your — friend — into many small pieces. Because who, among the so-civilized Terrestrials, can handle a sword?"

Gunli seemed to collapse. "O gods, O almighty gods — I didn't think of that —"

Suddenly she flung herself on Cerdic, tooth and nail and horns, snatching at his dagger. "Get him, Dominic!" she screamed. "Get him!"

The prince swept one brawny arm out. There was a dull smack and Gunli fell heavily to the floor.

"Now," grinned Cerdic, "choose your weapon!"

Flandry came forward and took one of the slender broadswords. Oddly, he was thinking mostly about the queen, huddled there on the floor. Poor kid, poor kid, she'd been under a greater strain than flesh and nerves were meant to bear. But give her a chance and she'd be all right.

Cerdic's eyes were almost dreamy now. He smiled as he crossed blades. "This will make up for a lot," he said. "Before you die, Terrestrial, you will no longer be a man —"

Steel rang in the great hall. Flandry parried the murderous slash and raked the prince's cheek. Cerdic roared and plunged, his blade weaving a net of death before him. Flandry skipped back, sword ringing on sword, shoulders to the wall.

They stood for an instant, straining blade against blade, sweat rivering off them, and bit by bit the Scothan's greater strength bent Flandry's arm aside. Suddenly the Terrestrial let go, striking out almost in the same moment, and the prince's steel hissed by his face.

He ran back and Cerdic rushed him again. The Scothan was wide open for the simplest stop thrust, but Flandry didn't want to kill him. They closed once more, blades clashing, and the human waited for his chance.

It came, an awkward move, and then one supremely skillful twist. Cerdic's sword went spinning out of his hand and across the room and the prince stood disarmed with Flandry's point at his throat.

For a moment he gaped in utter stupefaction. Flandry laughed harshly and said: "My dear friend, you forget that deliberate archaism is one characteristic of a decadent society. There's hardly a noble in the Empire who hasn't studied scientific fencing."

Defeat was heavy in the prince's defiant voice: "Kill me, then. Be done with it."

"There's been too much killing, and you can be too useful." Flandry threw his own weapon aside and cocked his fists. "But there's one thing I've wanted to do for a long, long time."

Despite the Scothan's powerful but clumsy defense, Flandry proceeded to beat the living hell out of him.

"We've saved Scotha, all Scotha," said Flandry. "Think, girl. What would have happened if you'd gone on into the Empire? Even if you'd won — and that was always doubtful, for Terra is mightier than you thought — you'd only have fallen into civil war. You just didn't have the capacity to run an empire — as witness the fact that your own allies and conquests turned on you the first chance they got. You'd have fought each other over the spoils, greater powers would have moved in, Scotha would have been ripe for sacking. Eventually you'd have gone down into Galactic oblivion. The present conflict was really quite small; it took far fewer lives than even a successful invasion of the Empire would have done. And now Terra will bring the peace you longed for, Gunli."

"Aye," she whispered. "We deserve to be conquered."

"But you aren't," he said. "The southerners hold Scotha now, and Terra will recognize them as the legal government — with you the queen, Gunli. You'll be another vassal state of the Empire, yes, but with all your freedoms except the liberty to rob and kill other races. And trade with the rest of the Empire will bring you a greater and more enduring prosperity than war ever would.

"I suppose that the Empire is decadent. But there's no reason why it can't some day have a renaissance. When the vigorous new peoples such as yours are guided by the ancient wisdom of Terra, the Galaxy may see its greatest glory."

She smiled at him. It was still a wan smile, but something of her old spirit was returning to her. "I don't think the Empire is so far gone, Dominic," she said. "Not when it has men like you." She took his hands. "And what will you be doing now?"

He met her eyes, and there was a sudden loneliness within him. She was very beautiful.

But it could never work out. Best to leave now, before a bright memory grew tarnished with the day-to-day clashing of personalities utterly foreign to each other. She would forget him in time, find someone else, and he — well —

"I have my work," he said.

They looked up to the bright sky. Far above them, the first of the descending Imperial ships glittered in the sunlight like a falling star.

Made in the USA
Lexington, KY
12 February 2010